THE
HUNDRED
PENNY BOX

In memory of my maternal grandparents:
RICHARD FRAZIER, SR.—great Black patriarch
And the woman he loved—his wife, MARY FRAZIER

This book is also for my brother:
JOHN W. BELL

THE HUNDRED PENNY BOX

Sharon Bell Mathis

Illustrated by Leo & Diane Dillon

Puffin Books

PUFFIN BOOKS

Published by the Penguin Group
Penguin Books USA Inc., 375 Hudson Street, New York, New York 10014, U.S.A.
Penguin Books Ltd, 27 Wrights Lane, London W8 5TZ, England
Penguin Books Australia Ltd, Ringwood, Victoria, Australia
Penguin Books Canada Ltd, 10 Alcorn Avenue, Toronto, Ontario, Canada M4V 3B2
Penguin Books (N.Z.) Ltd, 182–190 Wairau Road, Auckland 10, New Zealand

Penguin Books Ltd, Registered Offices: Harmondsworth, Middlesex, England
First published by Viking Penguin Inc. 1975
Published in Puffin Books 1986
17 19 20 18
Text copyright © Sharon Bell Mathis, 1975
Illustrations copyright © Leo and Diane Dillon, 1975
All rights reserved

Set in Palatino
Printed in the United States of America

"Take My Hand, Precious Lord" by Thomas A. Dorsey
Copyright © 1938 by Hill & Range Songs, Inc.
Copyright renewed, assigned to Unichappell Music, Inc.
(Rightsong Music, Publisher)
International copyright secured. All rights reserved. Used by permission

Library of Congress Cataloging in Publication Data
Mathis, Sharon Bell.   The hundred penny box.
Reprint. Originally published: New York: Viking Press, 1975.
Summary: Michael's love for his great-great-aunt,
who lives with them, leads him to intercede with his
mother, who wants to toss out all her old things.
[1. Grandmothers—Fiction.   2. Family life—Fiction]
I. Dillon, Leo, ill.   II. Dillon, Diane, ill.   III. Title.
PZ7.M4284Hu 1986   [E]   86-3293   ISBN 0-14-032169-1

In your shadow I have grown up. . . . And your beauty
strikes me to the heart like the flash of an eagle.

Leopold Sedar Senghor
Black Woman

Michael sat down on the bed that used to be his and watched his great-great-aunt, Aunt Dew, rocking in the rocking chair.

He wanted to play with the hundred penny box— especially since it was raining outside—but Aunt Dew was singing that long song again. Sometimes when she sang it she would forget who he was for a whole day.

Then she would call him John.

John was his father's name. Then his mother would say, "He's Mike, Aunt Dew. His name is Michael. John's name is John. His name is Michael." But if his father was home, Aunt Dew would just say "Where's my boy?" Then it was hard to tell whether she meant him or his father. And he would have to wait until she said something more before he knew which one she meant.

9

Aunt Dew didn't call his mother any name at all.

Michael had heard his father and mother talking in bed late one night. It was soon after they had come from going to Atlanta to bring back Aunt Dew. "She won't even look at me—won't call my name, nothing," his mother had said, and Michael could tell she had been crying. "She doesn't like me. I know it. I can tell. I do everything I can to make her comfortable—" His mother was crying hard. "I rode half the way across this city—all the way to Mama Dee's—to get some home-made ice cream, some decent ice cream. Mama Dee said, 'The ice cream be melted fore you get home.' So I took a cab back and made her lunch and gave her the ice cream. I sat down at the table and tried to drink my coffee—I mean, I wanted to talk to her, say something. But she sat there and ate that ice cream and looked straight ahead at the wall and never said nothing to me. She talks to Mike and if I come around she even stops talking sometime." His mother didn't say anything for a while and then he heard her say, "I care about her. But she's making me miserable in my own house."

Michael heard his father say the same thing he always said about Aunt Dew. "She's a one-hundred-year-old lady, baby." Sometimes his father would add,

"And when I didn't have nobody, she was there. Look here—after Big John and Junie drowned, she gave me a home. I didn't have one. I didn't have nothing. No mother, no father, no nobody. Nobody but her. I've loved her all my life. Like I love you. And that tough beautiful boy we made—standing right outside the door and listening for all he's worth—and he's supposed to be in his room sleep."

Michael remembered he had run back to his room and gotten back into bed and gotten up again and tiptoed over to the bedroom door to close it a little and shut off some of the light shining from the bathroom onto Aunt Dew's face. Then he looked at Aunt Dew and wished she'd wake up and talk to him like she did when she felt like talking and telling him all kinds of stories about people.

"Hold tight, Ruth," he had heard his father say that night. "She knows we want her. She knows it. And baby, baby—sweet woman, you doing fine. Everything you doing is right." Then Michael could hear the covers moving where his mother and father were and he knew his father was putting his arms around his mother because sometimes he saw them still asleep in the morning and that's the way they looked.

But he was tired of remembering now and he was tired of Aunt Dew singing and singing and singing.

"Aunt Dew," Michael whispered close to his great-great-aunt's wrinkled face. "Can we play with the hundred penny box?"

"Precious Lord—"

"Aunt Dew! Let's count the pennies out."

"Take my hand—"

"Aunt Dew!"

"Lead me on—"

Michael thought for a moment. He knew the large scratched wooden box was down beside the dresser, on the floor where he could easily get it.

Except it was no fun to count the pennies alone.

It was better when Aunt Dew whacked him a little and said, "Stop right there, boy. You know what that penny means?" And he'd say, "You tell me," and she would tell him.

But when she started singing it was hard to stop her. At least when she was dancing what she called "moving to the music," she'd get tired after a while. Then she would tell him about the pennies and help count them too.

Michael cupped his large hands—everybody talked

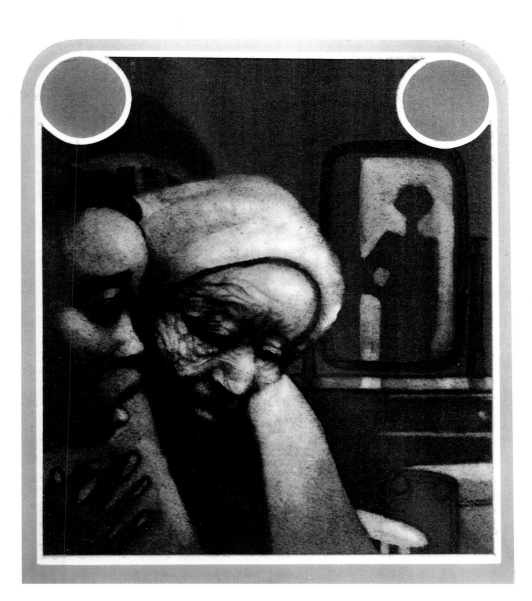

about how large his hands were for his age—around his great-great-aunt's ear. "Aunt Dew!" he said loudly.

Aunt Dew stopped rocking hard and turned and looked at him. But he didn't say anything and she didn't say anything. Aunt Dew turned her head and began to sing again. Exactly where she had left off. *"Let me stand—"*

Michael moved away from the rocking chair and sat back down on the bed. Then he got up and went to the dresser. He reached down and picked up the heavy, scratched-up hundred penny box from the floor, walked to the bedroom door, and stood there for a moment before he went out.

There was no way to stop Aunt Dew once she started singing that long song.

Michael walked down the hall and held the huge box against his stomach. He could still hear Aunt Dew's high voice.

"I am weak. I am worn."

"What's wrong?" his mother asked when he walked into the kitchen and sat down on a chair and stared at the floor.

He didn't want to answer.

14   "Oh," his mother said and reached for the hundred

penny box in his arms. "Give me that thing," she said. "That goes today! Soon as Aunt Dew's sleep, that goes in the furnace."

Michael almost jumped out of the chair. He wouldn't let go of the big, heavy box. He could hear his great-great-aunt's voice. She was singing louder. *"Lead me through the night, precious Lord. Take my hand."*

"You can't take the hundred penny box," Michael cried. "I'll tell Daddy if you take it and burn it up in the furnace like you burned up all the rest of Aunt Dew's stuff!" Then Michael thought of all the things he and Aunt Dew had hidden in his closet, and almost told his mother.

His mother walked closer to him and stood there but he wasn't afraid. Nobody was going to take Aunt Dew's hundred penny box. Nobody. Nobody. Nobody.

"Aunt Dew's like a child," his mother said quietly. "She's like you. Thinks she needs a whole lot of stuff she really doesn't. I'm not taking her pennies—you know I wouldn't take her pennies. I'm just getting rid of that big old ugly wooden box always under foot!"

Michael stood up. "No," he said.

"Mike, did you say no to me?" his mother asked. She put her hands on her hips.

"I mean," Michael said and tried to think fast. "Aunt Dew won't go to sleep if she doesn't see her box in the corner. Can I take it back and then you can let her see it? And when she goes to sleep, you can take it."

"Go put it back in her room then," his mother said. "I'll get it later."

"Okay," Michael said and held the heavy box tighter and walked slowly back down the hall to the small bedroom that used to be his. He opened the door and went in, put the hundred penny box down on the floor and sat down on it, staring at his aunt. She wasn't singing, just sitting. "John-boy," she said.

"Yes, Aunt Dew," Michael answered and didn't care this time that she was calling him John again. He was trying to think.

"Put my music on."

The music wasn't going to help him think because the first thing she was going to do was to make him "move" too.

But Michael got off the hundred penny box and reached under his bed and pulled out his blue record player that he had got for his birthday. He had already plugged it in the wall when he heard her say, "Get 16 mine. My own Victrola, the one your father give me."

"Momma threw it out," Michael said and knew he had told her already, a lot of times. "It was broken."

Aunt Dew squeezed her lips real tight together. "Your momma gonna throw me out soon," she said.

Michael stood still and stared at his great-great-aunt. "Momma can't throw *people* out," he said.

"Put my music on, boy," Aunt Dew said again. "And be quick about it."

"Okay," Michael said and turned the record player on and got the record, Aunt Dew's favorite, that they had saved and hidden in the bottom drawer.

The dusty, chipped record was of a lady singing that long song, *"Precious Lord, Take My Hand."* Michael turned it down low.

Aunt Dew started humming and Michael sat down on the bed and tried to think about what he'd do with the hundred penny box.

Aunt Dew got up from her rocking chair and stood up. She kept her arms down by her sides and made her thin hands into fists and clenched her lips tight and moved real slow in one spot. Her small shoulders just went up and down and up and down. "Get up, John-boy," she said, "and move with me. Move with Dew-bet Thomas!"

"I don't feel like dancing," Michael said and kept sitting on the bed. But he watched his great-great-aunt move both her thin arms to one side and then to the other and move her hands about and hold her dress. Then she stopped and started all of a sudden again, just swinging her arms and moving her shoulders up and down and singing some more. Every time the record ended, he'd start it again.

When he was playing it for the third time, he said, "Aunt Dew, where will you put your hundred pennies if you lose your hundred penny box?"

"When I lose my hundred penny box, I lose me," she said and kept moving herself from side to side and humming.

"I mean maybe you need something better than an old cracked-up, wacky-dacky box with the top broken."

"It's *my* old cracked-up, wacky-dacky box with the top broken," Aunt Dew said. And Michael saw her move her shoulders real high that time. "Them's my years in that box," she said. "That's me in that box."

"Can I hide the hundred penny box, Aunt Dew," Michael asked, hoping she'd say yes and not ask him why. He'd hide it like the other stuff she had asked him 19 to and had even told him where to hide it most of the time.

"No, don't hide my hundred penny box!" Aunt Dew said out loud. "Leave my hundred penny box right alone. Anybody takes my hundred penny box takes me!"

"Just in case," Michael said impatiently and wished his great-great-aunt would sit back down in her chair so he could talk to her. "Just in case Momma puts it in the furnace when you go to sleep like she puts all your stuff in the furnace in the basement."

"What your momma name?"

"Oh, no," Michael said. "You keep *on* forgetting Momma's name!" That was the only thing bad about being a hundred years old like Aunt Dew—you kept *on* forgetting things that were important.

"Hush, John-boy," Aunt Dew said and stopped dancing and humming and sat back down in the chair and put the quilt back over her legs.

"You keep on forgetting."

"I don't."

"You do, you keep on forgetting!"

"Do I forget to play with you when you worry me to death to play?"

Michael didn't answer.

"Do I forget to play when you want?"

"No."

"Okay. What your momma name? Who's that in my kitchen?"

"Momma's name is Ruth, but this isn't your house. Your house is in Atlanta. We went to get you and now you live with us."

"Ruth."

Michael saw Aunt Dew staring at him again. Whenever she stared at him like that, he never knew what she'd say next. Sometimes it had nothing to do with what they had been talking about.

"You John's baby," she said, still staring at him. "Look like John just spit you out."

"That's my father."

"My great-nephew," Aunt Dew said. "Only one ever care about me." Aunt Dew rocked hard in her chair then and Michael watched her. He got off the bed and turned off the record player and put the record back into the bottom drawer. Then he sat down on the hundred penny box again.

"See that tree out there?" Aunt Dew said and pointed her finger straight toward the window with the large 21

tree pressed up against it. Michael knew exactly what she'd say.

"Didn't have no puny-looking trees like that near my house," she said. "Dewbet Thomas—that's me, and Henry Thomas—that was my late husband, had the biggest, tallest, prettiest trees and the widest yard in all Atlanta. And John, that was your daddy, liked it most because he was city and my five sons, Henry, Jr., and Truke and Latt and the twins—Booker and Jay— well, it didn't make them no never mind because it was always there. But when my oldest niece Junie and her husband—we called him Big John—brought your daddy down to visit every summer, they couldn't get the suitcase in the house good before he was climbing up and falling out the trees. We almost had to feed him up them trees!"

"Aunt Dew, we have to hide the box."

"Junie and Big John went out on that water and I was feeling funny all day. Didn't know what. Just feeling funny. I told Big John, I said, 'Big John, that boat old. Nothing but a piece a junk.' But he fooled around and said, 'We taking it out.' I looked and saw him and Junie on that water. Then it wasn't nothing. Both gone. And the boat turned over, going downstream. Your daddy, brand-new little britches on, just standing there look- 23 ing, wasn't saying nothing. No hollering. I try to give him a big hunk of potato pie. But he just looking at me, just looking and standing. Wouldn't eat none of that pie. Then I said, 'Run get Henry Thomas and the boys.' He looked at me and then he looked at that water. He turned round real slow and walked toward the west field. He never run. All you could see was them stiff little britches—red they was—moving through the corn. Bare-waisted, he was. When we found the boat later, he took it clean apart—what was left of it—every plank, and pushed it back in that water. I watched him. Wasn't a piece left of that boat. Not a splinter.''

"Aunt Dew, where can we hide the box!''

"What box?''

"The hundred penny box.''

"We can't hide the hundred penny box and if she got to take my hundred penny box—she might as well take me!''

"We have to hide it!''

"No—'we' don't. It's *my* box!''

"It's *my* house. And I said we have to hide it!''

"How you going to hide a house, John?''

"Not the house! Our hundred penny box!''

24   "It's *my* box!''

Michael was beginning to feel desperate. But he couldn't tell her what his mother had said. "Suppose Momma takes it when you go to sleep?"

Aunt Dew stopped rocking and stared at him again. "Like John just spit you out," she said. "Go on count them pennies, boy. Less you worry me in my grave if you don't. Dewbet Thomas's hundred penny box. Dewbet Thomas a hundred years old and I got a penny to prove it—each year!"

Michael got off the hundred penny box and sat on the floor by his great-great-aunt's skinny feet stuck down inside his father's old slippers. He pulled the big wooden box toward him and lifted the lid and reached in and took out the small cloth roseprint sack filled with pennies. He dumped the pennies out into the box.

He was about to pick up one penny and put it in the sack, the way they played, and say "One," when his great-great-aunt spoke.

"Why you want to hide my hundred penny box?"

"To play," Michael said, after he thought for a moment.

"Play now," she said. "Don't hide my hundred penny box. I got to keep looking at my box and when I don't see my box I won't see me neither."

"One!" Michael said and dropped the penny back into the old print sack.

"18 and 74," Aunt Dew said. "Year I was born. Slavery over! Black men in Congress running things. They was in charge. It was the Reconstruction."

Michael counted twenty-seven pennies back into the old print sack before she stopped talking about Reconstruction. "19 and 01," Aunt Dew said. "I was twenty-seven years. Birthed my twin boys. Hattie said, 'Dewbet, you got two babies.' I asked Henry Thomas, I said 'Henry Thomas, what them boys look like?' "

By the time Michael had counted fifty-six pennies, his mother was standing at the door.

"19 and 30," Aunt Dew said. "Depression. Henry Thomas, that was my late husband, died. Died after he put the fifty-six penny in my box. He had the double pneumonia and no decent shoes and he worked too hard. Said he was going to sweat the trouble out his lungs. Couldn't do it. Same year I sewed that fancy dress for Rena Coles. She want a hundred bows all over that dress. I was sewing bows and tieing bows and twisting bows and cursing all the time. Was her *fourth* husband and she want a dress full of bow-ribbons.
26 Henry the one started that box, you know. Put the first

thirty-one pennies in it for me and it was my birthday. After fifty-six, I put them all in myself."

"Aunt Dew, time to go to bed," his mother said, standing at the door.

"Now, I'm not sleepy," Aunt Dew said. "John-boy and me just talking. Why you don't call him John? Look like John just spit him out. Why you got to call that boy something different from his daddy?"

Michael watched his mother walk over and open the window wide. "We'll get some fresh air in here," she said. "And then, Aunt Dew, you can take your nap better and feel good when you wake up." Michael wouldn't let his mother take the sack of pennies out of his hand. He held tight and then she let go.

"I'm not sleepy," Aunt Dew said again. "This child and me just talking."

"I know," his mother said, pointing her finger at him a little. "But we're just going to take our nap anyway."

"I got a long time to sleep and I ain't ready now. Just leave me sit here in this little narrow piece a room. I'm not bothering nobody."

"Nobody said you're bothering anyone but as soon as I start making that meat loaf, you're going to go to

sleep in your chair and fall out again and hurt yourself

and John'll wonder where I was and say I was on the telephone and that'll be something all over again."

"Well, I'll sit on the floor and if I fall, I'll be there already and it won't be nobody's business but my own."

"Michael," his mother said and took the sack of pennies out of his hand and laid it on the dresser. Then she reached down and closed the lid of the hundred penny box and pushed it against the wall. "Go out the room, honey, and let Momma help Aunt Dew into bed."

"I been putting Dewbet Thomas to bed a long time and I can still do it," Aunt Dew said.

"I'll just help you a little," Michael heard his mother say through the closed door.

As soon as his mother left the room, he'd go in and sneak out the hundred penny box.

But where would he hide it?

Michael went into the bathroom to think, but his mother came in to get Aunt Dew's washcloth. "Why are you looking like that?" she asked. "If you want to play go in my room. Play there, or in the living room. And don't go bothering Aunt Dew. She needs her rest."

Michael went into his father's and his mother's room and lay down on the big king bed and tried to think of a place to hide the box.

He had an idea!

He'd hide it down in the furnace room and sneak Aunt Dew downstairs to see it so she'd know where it was. Then maybe they could sit on the basement steps inside and play with it sometimes. His mother would never know. And his father wouldn't care as long as Aunt Dew was happy. He could even show Aunt Dew the big pipes and the little pipes.

Michael heard his mother close his bedroom door and walk down the hall toward the kitchen.

He'd tell Aunt Dew right now that they had a good place to hide the hundred penny box. The best place of all.

Michael got down from the huge bed and walked quietly back down the hall to his door and knocked on it very lightly. Too lightly for his mother to hear.

Aunt Dew didn't answer.

"Aunt Dew," he whispered after he'd opened the door and tiptoed up to the bed. "It's me. Michael."

Aunt Dew was crying.

Michael looked at his great-great-aunt and tried to say something but she just kept crying. She looked extra small in his bed and the covers were too close about her neck. He moved them down a little and then   31 her face didn't look so small. He waited to see if she'd stop crying but she didn't. He went out of the room and down the hall and stood near his mother. She was chopping up celery. "Aunt Dew's crying," he said.

"That's all right," his mother said. "Aunt Dew's all right."

"She's crying real hard."

"When you live long as Aunt Dew's lived, honey—sometimes you just cry. She'll be all right."

"She's not sleepy. You shouldn't make her go to sleep if she doesn't want to. Daddy never makes her go to sleep."

"You say you're not sleepy either, but you always go to sleep."

"Aunt Dew's bigger than me!"

"She needs her naps."

"Why?"

"Michael, go play please," his mother said. "I'm tired and I'm busy and she'll hear your noise and never go to sleep."

"She doesn't have to if she doesn't want!" Michael yelled and didn't care if he did get smacked. "We were just playing and then you had to come and make her cry!"

"Without a nap, she's irritable and won't eat. She has to eat. She'll get sick if she doesn't eat."

"You made her cry!" Michael yelled.

"Michael John Jefferson," his mother said too quietly. "If you don't get away from me and stop that yelling and stop that screaming and leave me alone—!"

Michael stood there a long time before he walked away.

"Mike," his mother called but he didn't answer. All he did was stop walking.

His mother came down the hall and put her arm about him and hugged him a little and walked him back into the kitchen.

Michael walked very stiffly. He didn't feel like any hugging. He wanted to go back to Aunt Dew.

"Mike," his mother said, leaning against the counter and still holding him.

Michael let his mother hold him but he didn't hold her back. All he did was watch the pile of chopped celery.

"Mike, I'm going to give Aunt Dew that tiny mahogany chest your daddy made in a woodshop class when he was a teen-ager. It's really perfect for that little sack of pennies and when she sees it on that pretty dresser 33

scarf she made—the one I keep on her dresser—she'll like it just as well as that big old clumsy box. She won't even miss that big old ugly thing!"

"The hundred penny box isn't even *bothering* you!"

His mother didn't answer. But Michael heard her sigh. "You don't even care about Aunt Dew's stuff," Michael yelled a little. He even pulled away from his mother. He didn't care at all about her hugging him. Sometimes it seemed to him that grown-ups never cared about anything unless it was theirs and nobody else's. He wasn't going to be like that when he grew up and could work and could do anything he wanted to do.

"Mike," his mother said quietly. "Do you remember that teddy bear you had? The one with the crooked head? We could never sit him up quite right because of the way you kept him bent all the time. You'd bend him up while you slept with him at night and bend him up when you hugged him, played with him. Do you remember that, Mike?"

Why did she have to talk about a dumb old teddy bear!

"You wouldn't let us touch that teddy bear. I mean it was all torn up and losing its stuffing all over the place. 34 And your daddy wanted to get rid of it and I said, 'No.

Mike will let us know when he doesn't need that teddy bear anymore.' So you held onto that teddy bear and protected it from all kinds of monsters and people. Then, one day, you didn't play with it anymore. I think it was when little Corky moved next door."

"Corky's not little!"

"I'm sorry. Yes—Corky's big. He's a very big boy. But Corky wasn't around when you and I cleaned up your room a little while back. We got rid of a lot of things so that Aunt Dew could come and be more comfortable. That day, you just tossed that crooked teddy bear on top of the heap and never even thought about it—"

"I *did* think about it," Michael said.

"But you knew you didn't need it anymore," his mother whispered and rubbed his shoulder softly. "But it's not the same with Aunt Dew. She will hold onto everything that is hers—just to hold onto them! She will hold them tighter and tighter and she will not go forward and try to have a new life. This is a new life for her, Mike. You must help her have this new life and not just let her go backward to something she can never go back to. Aunt Dew does *not* need that huge, broken, half-rotten wooden box that you stumble all over the house with—just to hold one tiny little sack of pennies!"

"I don't stumble around with it!"

His mother reached down then and kissed the top of his head. "You're the one that loves that big old box, Mike. I think that's it."

Michael felt the kiss in his hair and he felt her arms about him and he saw the pile of celery. His mother didn't understand. She didn't understand what a hundred penny box meant. She didn't understand that a new life wasn't very good if you had to have everything old taken away from you—just for a dumb little stupid old funny-looking ugly little red box, a shiny ugly nothing box that didn't even look like it was big enough to hold a sack of one hundred pennies!

Mike put his arms around his mother. Maybe he could make her understand. He hugged her hard. That's what she had done—hugged him. "All Aunt Dew wants is her hundred penny box," Michael said. "That's the only thing——"

"And all you wanted was that teddy bear," his mother answered.

"You can't burn it," Michael said and moved away from his mother. "You can't burn any more of Aunt 37

Dew's stuff. You can't take the hundred penny box. I said you can't take it!"

"Okay," his mother said.

Michael went down the hall and opened the door to his room.

"No, Mike," his mother said and hurried after him. "Don't go in there now."

"I am," Michael said.

His mother snatched him and shut the door and pulled him into the living room and practically threw him into the stuffed velvet chair. "You're as stubborn as your father," she said. "Everything your way or else!" She was really angry. "Just sit there," she said. "And don't move until I tell you!"

As soon as Michael heard his mother chopping celery again, he got up from the chair.

He tiptoed into his room and shut the door without a sound.

Aunt Dew was staring at the ceiling. There was perspiration on her forehead and there was water in the dug-in places around her eyes.

"Aunt Dew?"

"What you want, John-boy?"

"I'm sorry Momma's mean to you."

"Ain't nobody mean to Dewbet Thomas—cause Dewbet Thomas ain't mean to nobody," Aunt Dew said, and reached her hand out from under the cover and patted Michael's face. "Your Momma Ruth. She move around and do what she got to do. First time I see her—I say, 'John, she look frail but she ain't.' He said, 'No, she ain't frail.' I make out like I don't see her all the time." Aunt Dew said, and winked her eye. "But she know I see her. If she think I don't like her that ain't the truth. Dewbet Thomas like everybody. But me and her can't talk like me and John talk—cause she don't know all what me and John know."

"I closed the door," Michael said. "You don't have to sleep if you don't want to."

"I been sleep all day, John," Aunt Dew said.

Michael leaned over his bed and looked at his great-great-aunt. "You haven't been sleep all day," he said. "You've been sitting in your chair and talking to me and then you were dancing to your record and then we were counting pennies and we got to fifty-six and then Momma came."

"Where my hundred penny box?"

"I got it," Michael answered.

"Where you got it?"

"Right here by the bed."

"Watch out while I sleep."

He'd tell her about the good hiding place later. "Okay," he said.

Aunt Dew was staring at him. "Look like John just spit you out," she said.

Michael moved away from her. He turned his back and leaned against the bed and stared at the hundred penny box. All of a sudden it looked real *real* old and beat up.

"Turn round. Let me look at you."

Michael turned around slowly and looked at his great-great-aunt.

"John!"

"It's me," Michael said. "Michael."

He went and sat down on the hundred penny box.

"Come here so I can see you," Aunt Dew said.

Michael didn't move.

"Stubborn like your daddy. Don't pay your Aunt Dew no never mind!"

Michael still didn't get up.

"Go on back and do your counting out my pennies. Start with fifty-seven—where you left off. 19 and 31. Latt married that schoolteacher. We roasted three pigs.   41

Just acting the fool, everybody. Latt give her a pair of yellow shoes for her birthday. Walked off down the road one evening just like you please, she did. Had on them yellow shoes. Rode a freight train clean up to Chicago. Left his food on the table and all his clothes ironed. Six times she come back and stay for a while and then go again. Truke used to say, 'Wouldn't be *my* wife.' But Truke never did marry nobody. Only thing he care about was that car. He would covered it with a raincoat when it rained, if he could.''

"First you know me, then you don't,'' Michael said.

"Michael John Jefferson what your name is,'' Aunt Dew said. "Should be plain John like your daddy and your daddy's daddy—stead of all this new stuff. Name John and everybody saying 'Michael.' '' Aunt Dew was smiling. "Come here, boy,'' she said. "Come here close. Let me look at you. Got a head full of hair.''

Michael got up from the hundred penny box and stood at the foot of the bed.

"Get closer,'' Aunt Dew said.

Michael did.

"Turn these covers back little more. This little narrow piece a room don't have the air the way my big house did.''

42

"I took a picture of your house," Michael said and turned the covers back some more.

"My house bigger than your picture," Aunt Dew said. "Way bigger."

Michael leaned close to her on his bed and propped his elbows up on the large pillow under her small head. "Tell me about the barn again," he said.

"Dewbet and Henry Thomas had the biggest, reddest barn in all Atlanta, G-A!"

"And the swing Daddy broke," Michael asked and put his head down on the covers. Her chest was so thin under the thick quilt that he hardly felt it. He reached up and pushed a few wispy strands of her hair away from her closed eyes.

"Did more pulling it down than he did swinging."

"Tell me about the swimming pool," Michael said. He touched Aunt Dew's chin and covered it up with only three fingers.

It was a long time before Aunt Dew answered. "Wasn't no swimming pool," she said. "I done told you was a creek. Plain old creek. And your daddy like to got bit by a cottonmouth."

"Don't go to sleep, Aunt Dew," Michael said. "Let's talk."

44   "I'm tired, John."

"I can count the pennies all the way to the end if you want me to."

"Go head and count."

"When your hundred and one birthday comes, I'm going to put in the new penny like you said."

"Yes, John."

Michael reached up and touched Aunt Dew's eyes. "I have a good place for the hundred penny box, Aunt Dew," he said quietly.

"Go way. Let me sleep," she said.

"You wish you were back in your own house, Aunt Dew?"

"I'm going back," Aunt Dew said.

"You sad?"

"Hush, boy!"

Michael climbed all the way up on the bed and put his whole self alongside his great-great-aunt. He touched her arms. "Are your arms a hundred years old?" he asked. It was their favorite question game.

"Um-hm," Aunt Dew murmured and turned a little away from him.

Michael touched her face. "Is your face and your eyes and fingers a hundred years old too?"

"John, I'm tired," Aunt Dew said. "Don't talk so."

"How do you get to be a hundred years old?" Mi- 45

chael asked and raised up from the bed on one elbow and waited for his great-great-aunt to answer.

"First you have to have a hundred penny box," his great-great-aunt finally said.

"Where you get it from?" Michael asked.

"Somebody special got to give it to you," Aunt Dew said. "And soon as they give it to you, you got to be careful less it disappear."

"Aunt Dew—"

"Precious Lord—"

"Aunt Dew?"

"Take my hand—"

Michael put his head down on Aunt Dew's thin chest beneath the heavy quilt and listened to her sing her long song.

ABOUT THE AUTHOR

SHARON BELL MATHIS was born in Atlantic City, New Jersey, and grew up in Bedford Stuyvesant, Brooklyn. A graduate of Morgan State College in Baltimore, she recently received her Master of Library Science degree from Catholic University in Washington, D.C. For many years Mrs. Mathis was a special education teacher in junior high schools in Washington. She also writes a monthly column for *Ebony, Jr!*

Mrs. Mathis is the author of several books for young people, including *Sidewalk Story*, which received an award from the Council on Interracial Books for Children, and *Teacup Full of Roses*, which was an ALA Notable Book. Her most recent book for Viking was *Listen for the Fig Tree*, also an ALA Notable Book.

Sharon Bell Mathis lives in Washington with her family and a German shepherd named Candy Cane Mathis.

ABOUT THE ILLUSTRATORS

LEO and DIANE DILLON met when they were both students at the Parsons School of Design. Shortly after their marriage they resigned from their respective jobs to do free-lance illustrating. Several years later they began their successful collaboration as illustrators of children's books.

The Dillons live in a brownstone in Brooklyn, New York, with their young son Lee, who plays the guitar.

ABOUT THE BOOK

The art for this book was rendered with water colors applied with cotton. The light areas were created with water and bleach applied with a brush, and some areas were softened with the use of an air brush. Air brush was also used to create the frames for each picture. The art work was separated and reproduced in two colors. The text type is 14-point Palatino; the display type is Augustea.